The Treasure-Hunt Three
and
Judge Mia's Decree

By Brenda Darnley Martin
Illustrated by Rosemary Rowan Tyler

Brenda Darnley Martin

The Treasure-Hunt Three and Judge Mia's Decree

ISBN: 978-1-61170-004-6

First Printing
Proudly conceived, written, illustrated and
Printed in the United States of America

BrenMar Communications, LLC
P.O. Box 270352
Tampa, FL 33688-0352
www.brenmarcommunications.com

Robertson Publishing
59 N. Santa Cruz Avenue, Suite B
Los Gatos, California 95030 USA
(888) 354-5957 • www.RobertsonPublishing.com

This book is dedicated to
the memory of Tampa Police Officers
Jeffrey Kocab and David Curtis
and their brave comrades in law enforcement,
who serve to protect us all from bullying.

Other books in the Treasure-Hunt Fish Book Series:

Freddie, Hector and Tish: The Treasure-Hunt Fish

The Treasure-Hunt Fish And Miss Bernadette's Wish

To schedule an author visit
or for more information on these and future books, go to:
www.treasurehuntfish.com.

To purchase additional copies of this book go to:
www.rp–author.com/treasurehunt

Sweet dreams were dancing through Freddie's head
When his old Auntie May pulled back his bedspread.

"Rise and shine," she said, kissing his face,
"you don't want to be late to your special place!"

Old Tampa Bay was coming to light
As the sun chased away the darkness of night.

Hector and Tish would be on their way
To meet Freddie for another adventurous day.

He grabbed his backpack,
then kissed Auntie May.

And sped off to join them out in the bay.

Meeting at their designated place,
They took off quickly — as if in a race!
Faster and faster they swam out to sea,
'Til they came within sight of the great Carrie Lee.

Hector raced out ahead and was practically there,
When a school of Bull Sharks came out of nowhere!

As they circled around him, his heart filled with fear,
Their evil intentions becoming quite clear.

Realizing they were much larger than he,
Hector frantically searched for a chance to get free.

Alas, he was stuck and they kept him contained —
Taunting and teasing and calling him names.

But Freddie and Tish knew just what to do,
And quickly swam off to get Officer Muldoon.

Muldoon was an octopus with the local police.
Surely he'd manage to win Hector's release!

Officer Muldoon went with them right away
And in no time at all, held the sharks at bay.

As an octopus, you see,
he was the long arm of the law —
And with eight long arms, he didn't need claws!

Soon he had sent the sharks off to his jail
Where they gnashed their sharp teeth and continued
to wail.

"Don't ye sharks worry —
ye'll have yer day in court!"
The officer bellowed as he filled out his report.

And to prove he would do just what he said,
He took them to see Judge Mia Mendez.

Judge Mia was not only honest and fair,
But very revered in her judge's chair.

When the sharks were brought up in front of her bench
They grew frightened themselves and started to flinch.

The judge listened intently to both sides of the case
Then reached her decision and gave it post-haste.

"Bullying is not something we will allow,"
She said smiling at Hector, who was still cowering down.

"The sharks must apologize and make their amends;
Volunteer to help others; learn to be friends.

The bay is beautiful — there is plenty for all;
No need to torment and create useless brawls."

The sharks looked relieved and did as she said,
Realizing they could have stayed in trouble instead.

As the trio swam back to their homes in the bay,
They reflected on the events of the day.

Hector was grateful his friends were so bright —
And rushed to get help, not give into fright.

Freddie and Tish were glad he was well,
And at the same time, very proud of themselves.

They realized that true friendship means standing tall
And that safety for one is safety for all!

LaVergne, TN USA
22 October 2010
201731LV00002B